DATE DUE

PRINTED IN U.S.A.

For Lucy, who makes every Christmas the best one ever.

STERLING CHILDREN'S BOOKS
New York

An Imprint of Sterling Publishing Co., Inc.
1166 Avenue of the Americas
New York, NY 10036

First Sterling edition published in 2016. First published in 2015 by Macmillan Children's Books, an imprint of Pan Macmillan, a division of Macmillan Publishers International Limited. 20 New Wharf Road, London N1 9RR. Associated companies throughout the world www.panmacmillan.com

© 2015 by Ben Mantle

ISBN 978-1-4549-2121-9

For information about custom editions, special sales, and premium and corporate purchases, please contact Sterling Special Sales at 800-805-5489 or specialsales@sterlingpublishing.com.

Manufactured in China

Lot #:
2 4 6 8 10 9 7 5 3 1
07/16

www.sterlingpublishing.com

The Best Christmas Present Ever!

Ben Mantle

STERLING CHILDREN'S BOOKS

New York

Bear had a funny feeling he had forgotten something.

He'd already washed behind his ears,

and shampooed and styled his fur.

He just couldn't remember what it was. Maybe a walk would help.

Bear had just left his house when he bumped into his best friend, Squirrel.

"FOUR DAYS TILL CHRISTMAS!" shouted Squirrel excitedly. "I've got you such a great gift, Bear. I can't wait to give it to you!"

To: Bear
From: Squirrel

Oh no! Bear had forgotten to get Squirrel a present.

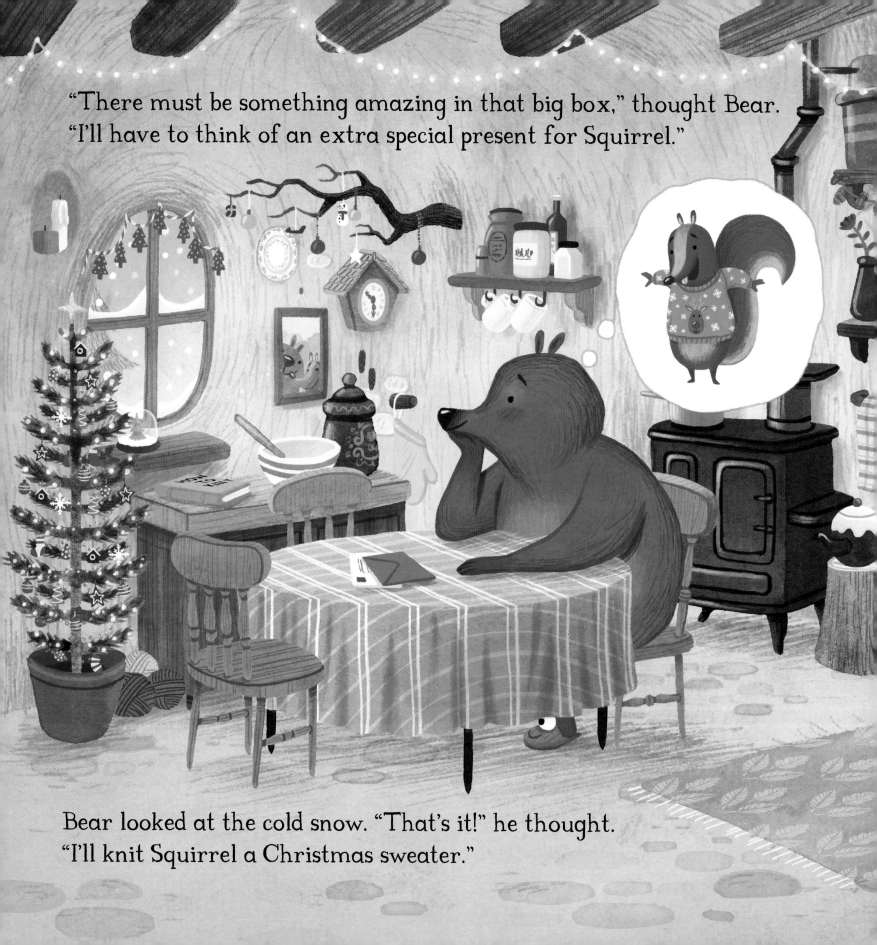

"There must be something amazing in that big box," thought Bear. "I'll have to think of an extra special present for Squirrel."

Bear looked at the cold snow. "That's it!" he thought. "I'll knit Squirrel a Christmas sweater."

He knitted all day,
clickity-click,

and all night,
clickity-clack,
until the sweater
was finished.

There was just one *tiny* problem . . .

Bear was not very good at knitting.

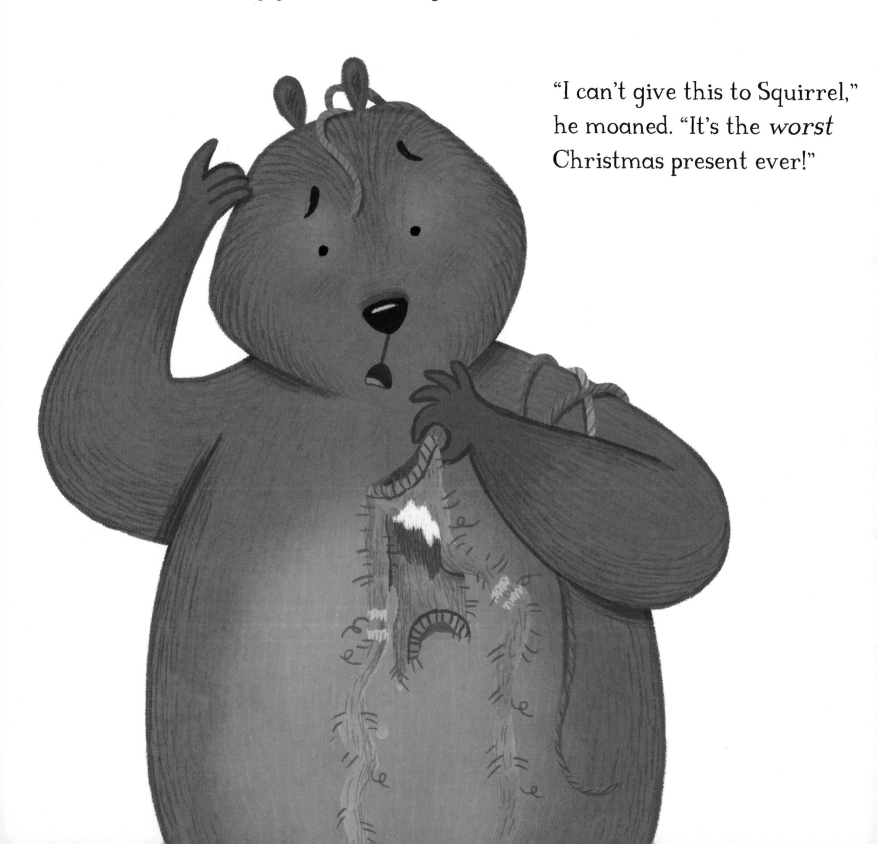

"I can't give this to Squirrel," he moaned. "It's the *worst* Christmas present ever!"

Now there were only THREE DAYS till Christmas.
Bear was feeling worried.

"Owl will know what to give Squirrel," thought Bear.

"Why don't you paint Squirrel a picture?" suggested Owl when
Bear paid him a visit.
"What a brilliant idea!" said Bear. "I will paint him a portrait."

Bear rushed home and got to work.

He painted all day, **splash,**

and all night, **splat,** until the painting was complete.

It was absolutely . . .

TERRIBLE!

Now there were only TWO DAYS till Christmas.
What was Bear going to do? Maybe Fox would know.

"It's nearly Christmas," Bear groaned to Fox later
that day.
"I know, exciting!" said Fox. "Have a slice of cake."
"But I don't know what to give Squirrel," Bear sighed.
He sat by the fire and thought . . .

"I know! I'll build him a rocking chair like this one," Bear decided.

Bear rushed out and collected a big pile of wood.

He spent all day sawing, scritch-scratch,

and all night hammering,
tap-tap-BANG.

Then he added the finishing touch . . .

CRUNCH! What a calamity!

There was only ONE DAY left till Christmas and Bear still had nothing to give Squirrel.

He threw the pieces of chair onto the pile of ruined presents.

Suddenly Bear was struck by a fantastic idea.
Squirrel was going to love it!

There were no days left.
Christmas had arrived!
Bear and Squirrel were having
a fabulous time drinking
hot chocolate and singing
their favorite songs.

But they couldn't wait any longer to open their presents.
"I'm going first!" said Bear, leading Squirrel outside.

"Ooh, what could it be?" asked Squirrel as he pulled off the wrapping.

"A sled!" he squealed. "This is the best Christmas present *ever!*"

"Thank you, Bear," Squirrel shouted. "Jump on!"

But there wasn't quite enough room for two.

"Maybe I should get your present," mumbled Squirrel.

Squirrel ran off and came back with the box.
"Merry Christmas, Bear!" he smiled.
Bear untied the ribbon excitedly and looked inside.

"It's empty," said Bear.
"All the best boxes are empty,"
replied Squirrel. "Just imagine
the things we can do with it!"

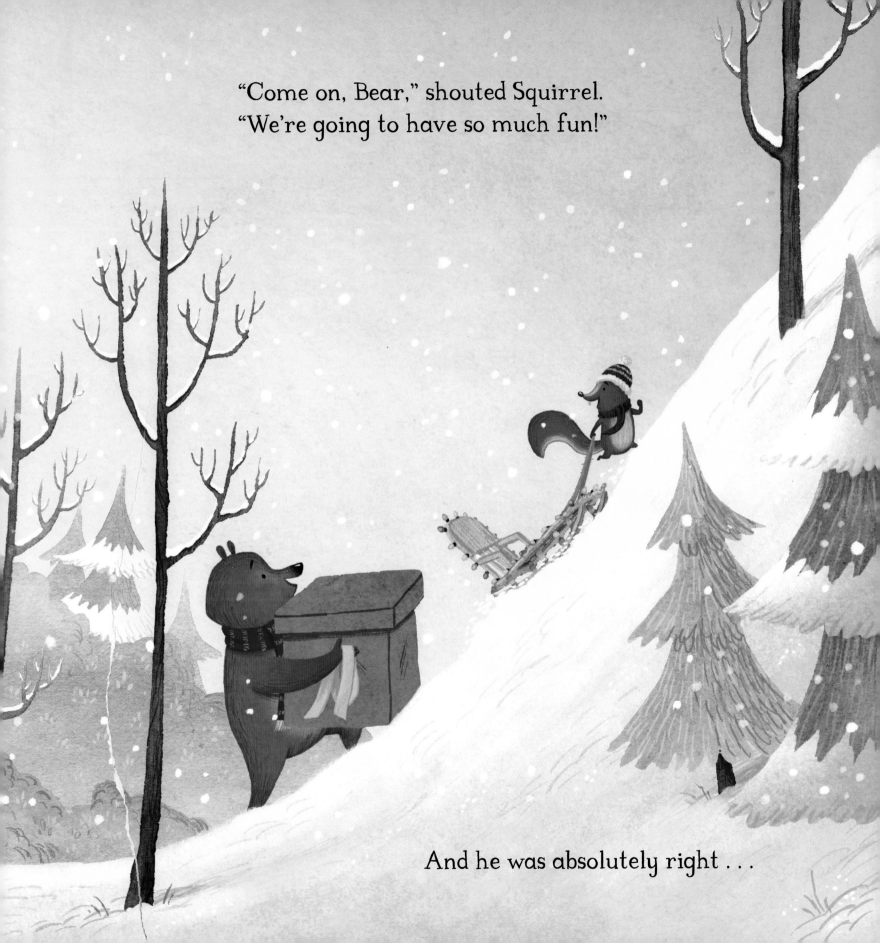

"Come on, Bear," shouted Squirrel.
"We're going to have so much fun!"

And he was absolutely right . . .

because now they BOTH had
the best Christmas presents ever.